my spring robin

BY ANNE ROCKWELL

ILLUSTRATED BY HARLOW ROCKWELL AND LIZZY ROCKWELL

ALADDIN · New York · London · Toronto · Sydney · New Delhi

For Dr. Mike Marino

🪔 ALADDIN

An imprint of Simon & Schuster Children's Publishing Division
1230 Avenue of the Americas, New York, NY 10020
First Aladdin hardcover edition February 2015
Copyright © 1987 by Anne Rockwell and Harlow Rockwell
Jacket illustration © 2015 by Lizzy Rockwell
All rights reserved, including the right of reproduction in whole or in part in any form.
ALADDIN is a trademark of Simon & Schuster, Inc., and related logo is a registered
trademark of Simon & Schuster, Inc.
For information about special discounts for bulk purchases, please contact Simon & Schuster
Special Sales at 1-866-506-1949 or business@simonandschuster.com.
The Simon & Schuster Speakers Bureau can bring authors to your live event. For more
information or to book an event contact the Simon & Schuster Speakers Bureau at
1-866-248-3049 or visit our website at www.simonspeakers.com.
Designed by Jessica Handelman
The text of this book was set in Kindergarten.
The illustrations for this book were rendered in pencil and watercolor.
Manufactured in China 0115 SCP
10 9 8 7 6 5 4 3 2 1
Library of Congress Control Number 2014943086
ISBN 978-1-4814-1137-0
ISBN 978-1-4814-1403-6 (eBook)
With appreciation and thanks to the Children's Literature Research Collections,
University of Minnesota Libraries, Minneapolis, for use of Harlow Rockwell's original
My Spring Robin artwork.

A robin sang a song for me
every day last summer.
I liked that robin.

But in the fall
my robin flew away.
My father said
it would come back
in the spring.
So when spring came,

I went looking for my spring robin.

I saw a bee
taking honey from a crocus,
but I didn't see my robin.

I looked into the yellow forsythia bush,

but my robin wasn't there.

My robin was not sitting
high up in the branches
of the magnolia tree.

In the fern garden
behind our outdoor table,

fuzzy fiddleheads were sprouting
in last year's wet, brown leaves.

But I didn't see
my robin there.

I saw a tiny toad.
It hopped behind
a clump of daffodils
to hide from me.

I looked high up into the sky
to see if my robin
was flying back to me.
Drops of rain fell on my face,
and our neighbor's cat ran home.

After the shower I picked
a little bunch of purple violets
for my mother.
I watched a shiny earthworm
wriggle up out of the ground.

And then I heard it.
I heard that song!
"Cheer-up, cheerilee!
Cheer-up, cheerilee!
Cheer-up, cheerilee!"
I knew who was singing that song!

It was my spring robin!